THIS BOOK BELONGS TO

~~Shaun~~   ~~Polly~~

....

....

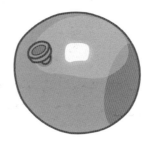

LADYBIRD BOOKS

UK | USA | Canada | Ireland | Australia | India | New Zealand | South Africa

Ladybird Books is part of the Penguin Random House group of companies
whose addresses can be found at global.penguinrandomhouse.com.

www.penguin.co.uk   www.puffin.co.uk   www.ladybird.co.uk

Penguin
Random House
UK

First published in Australia by Puffin Books, 2021
This edition published in Great Britain by Ladybird Books Ltd, 2022
001

LU DO   **BBC STUDIOS**

Printed in Great Britain

The authorized representative in the EEA is Penguin Random House Ireland,
Morrison Chambers, 32 Nassau Street, Dublin D02 YH68

A CIP catalogue record for this book is available from the British Library

ISBN: 978-0-241-55066-3

All correspondence to:
Ladybird Books, Penguin Random House Children's
One Embassy Gardens, 8 Viaduct Gardens, London SW11 7BW

FSC
www.fsc.org

MIX
Paper from
responsible sources
FSC® C018179

BLUEY

MUM SCHOOL

Bluey and Mum are in the lounge room playing with lots of balloons. Suddenly, Bingo runs through in her towel, chased by Dad!

"Hey, Bingo. Good work for having a bath," says Mum.
"Yeah, but she hasn't cleaned her teeth!" complains Dad.

It's Bluey's bathtime, too.
"I can smell you from
here," jokes Mum.

But Bluey wants to play Mum School with the balloons
as her children. Their names are . . .

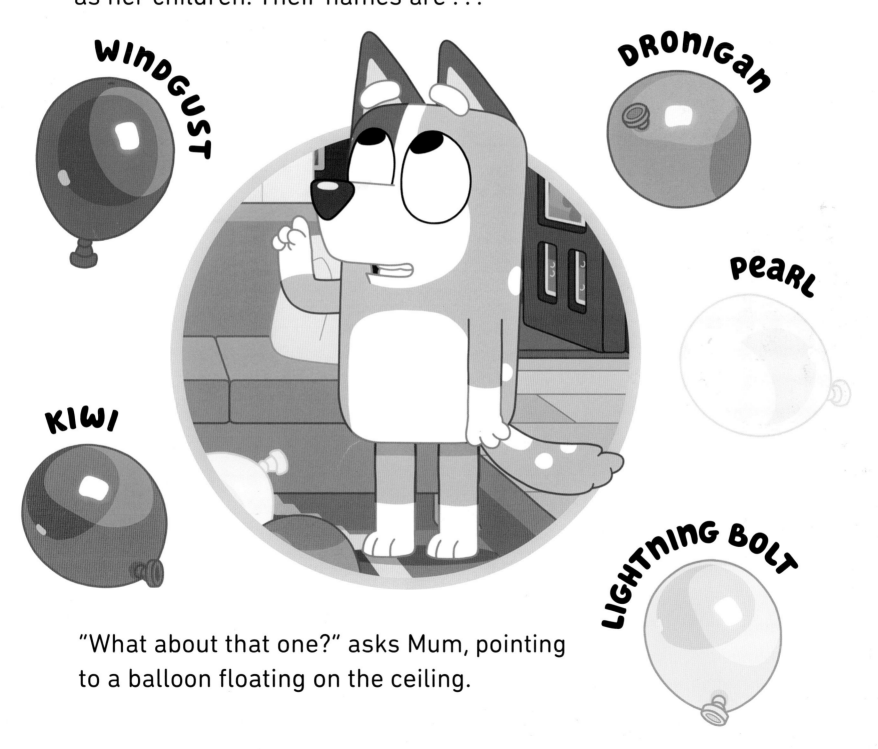

WINDGUST

DRONIGAH

PEARL

KIWI

LIGHTNING BOLT

"What about that one?" asks Mum, pointing
to a balloon floating on the ceiling.

"Oh, Greenie, **you're such a pickle!**" says Bluey, grabbing him with a robot claw.

Mum still wants to run the bath, but Bluey hands her a clipboard to record Bluey's score for being a good mum.

"You don't need someone keeping score," says Mum.
But, when Greenie escapes to the ceiling again and Bluey throws
a cushion at him, Mum changes her mind.
Now it's movie time for the kids. Two points to Bluey when she
suggests Greenie holds her hand so he doesn't fly away again!
He's such a handful.

Mum gives Bluey **zero points** for putting a cushion on Greenie's head.

Two points for telling off Windgust for calling Greenie a "cushion head".

Zero points for allowing Greenie to hit Windgust to get him back.

The kids are getting a bit out of control. "Maybe it's time for some exercise in the indoor pool," suggests Mum.
But Bluey has trouble making them walk along the hallway.
"It's frustrating when they don't listen to you," sighs Bluey.
"Yes, it is!" agrees Mum.

Maybe Bluey can show them how to walk properly . . .

"I'll show them all right," Bluey says, boinking
them with a roll of wrapping paper.
Zero points from Mum.

"Come on, Greenie. You're old enough to walk by yourself," says Bluey.
"Greenie finds walking a little tricky," explains Mum.
"Oh, nonsense," says Bluey. "This way!"

Bluey puts all the kids into the pool . . .
except Greenie.

"Now, Greenie, if I let you out of there, are you going to behave yourself?" asks Bluey.

"I think you know the answer," says Mum, raising an eyebrow. But other than giving Greenie a boink with the wrapping paper, Bluey doesn't know what to do.

Before Mum can offer any advice, they hear Dad and Bingo coming in.

"I just have to mark this other student. He's in Dad School," explains Mum, as they hide in the shower.

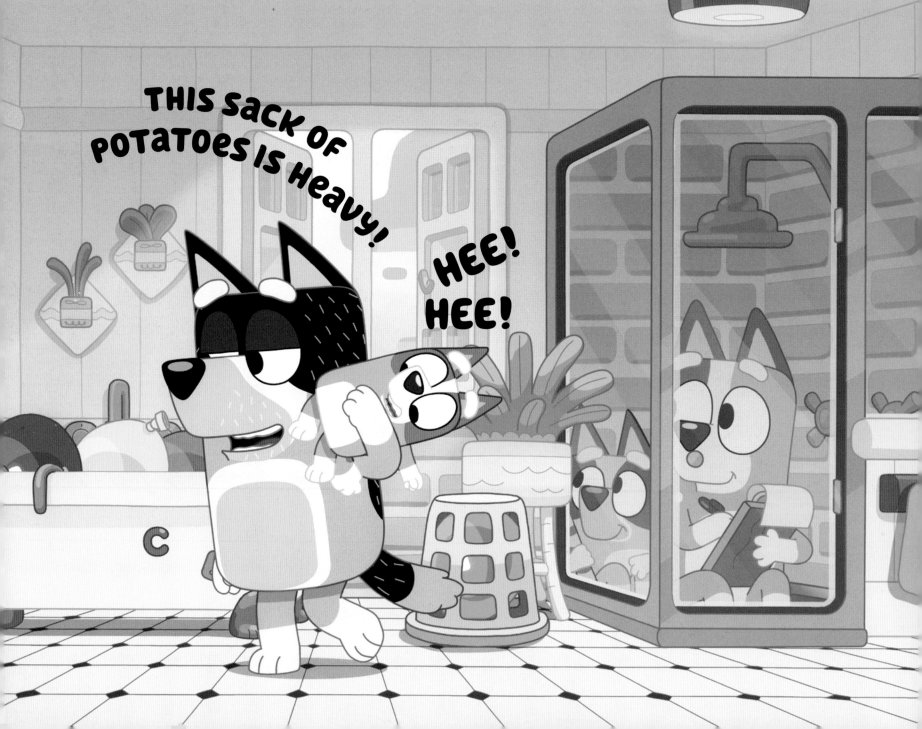

Dad is still trying to get Bingo to brush her teeth.
"Put me down," yells Bingo, squirming out of Dad's grip
and running away.

Dad gets **two points** for making it fun.

HEE! HEE!

Zero points when he gets distracted and Bingo slips away again.

And he gets **five points** for the tickling move!

UNHAND ME!

I DON'T WANT TO CLEAN MY TEETH!

But then Dad stops and examines Bingo. "Hmm. There must be a reason why you're being such a **pickle** tonight," Dad says.
He wonders if Bingo is still hungry.

"I'll race you to the kitchen," Dad exclaims.

GO!

"Wackadoo!" Mum gasps, giving him top marks.
Bluey's impressed. Maybe she can have
another go at dealing with Greenie.

Bluey takes Greenie out
of the basket, holding
him gently.
"Hi, sweetheart. There
must be a reason you
keep floating off."
Bluey wonders what
it could be . . .

Maybe Greenie just likes exploring! But he's not old enough to go exploring on his own yet.
"One day you can float up as high as you want. But for now here's a special present so you don't go too far." Bluey ties a magnet to Greenie's string to keep him down.

"Because I love you so much," says Bluey.

And that's worth **full marks** at Mum School.

Finally Bluey jumps in the pool with the kids for a splash!

After the bath, it's time to get dry.
"There you go, darlings," says Bluey,
patting her kids with a towel.
She's almost passed Mum School.

Bluey wants a go with the hairdryer, sending the kids flying everywhere . . .

But one kid floats all the way out of the door for an adventure – Greenie.

"Does this mean I fail Mum School?" asks Bluey, disappointed.
"Yeah, but that's OK. We all fail Mum School sometimes.
We can just start again tomorrow," says Mum.

"Will Greenie be OK?" asks Bluey.
"Yeah, I think he'll do just fine," replies Mum.
"How do you know?" asks Bluey, still unsure.

"Because he's got
a good mum."